D1476151

All about TEACHERS

Jennifer Boothroyd

Lerner Publications ◆ Minneapolis

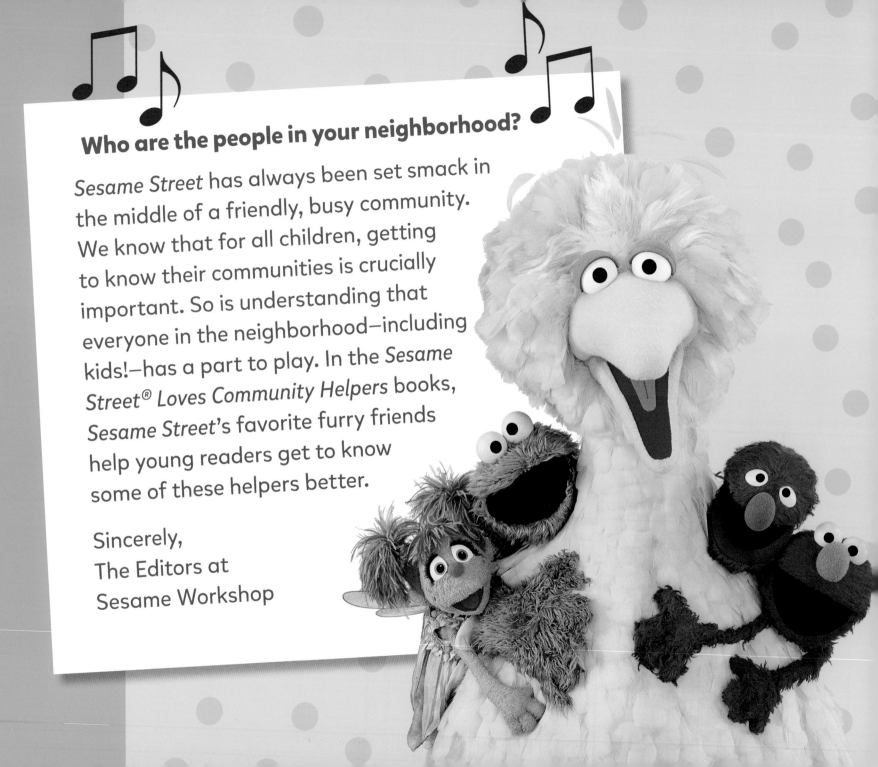

Who are the people in your neighborhood?

Sesame Street has always been set smack in the middle of a friendly, busy community. We know that for all children, getting to know their communities is crucially important. So is understanding that everyone in the neighborhood—including kids!—has a part to play. In the *Sesame Street® Loves Community Helpers* books, *Sesame Street*'s favorite furry friends help young readers get to know some of these helpers better.

Sincerely,
The Editors at
Sesame Workshop

Table of Contents

Teachers Are Terrific!

I love my teachers. They let me ask questions. Teachers make learning fun!

Why We Love Teachers

Teachers make the community a better place.

Teachers help us learn many things. They help keep us safe.

Teachers work in schools. Some schools are big, and some are small.

My school is small.

Teachers work with students in a classroom.

Teachers use many tools.

Sometimes we play learning games on a computer.

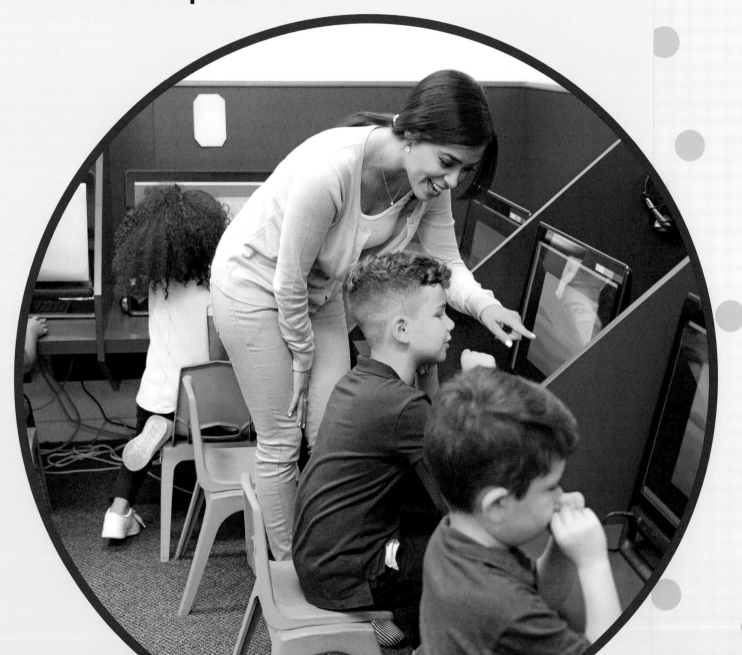

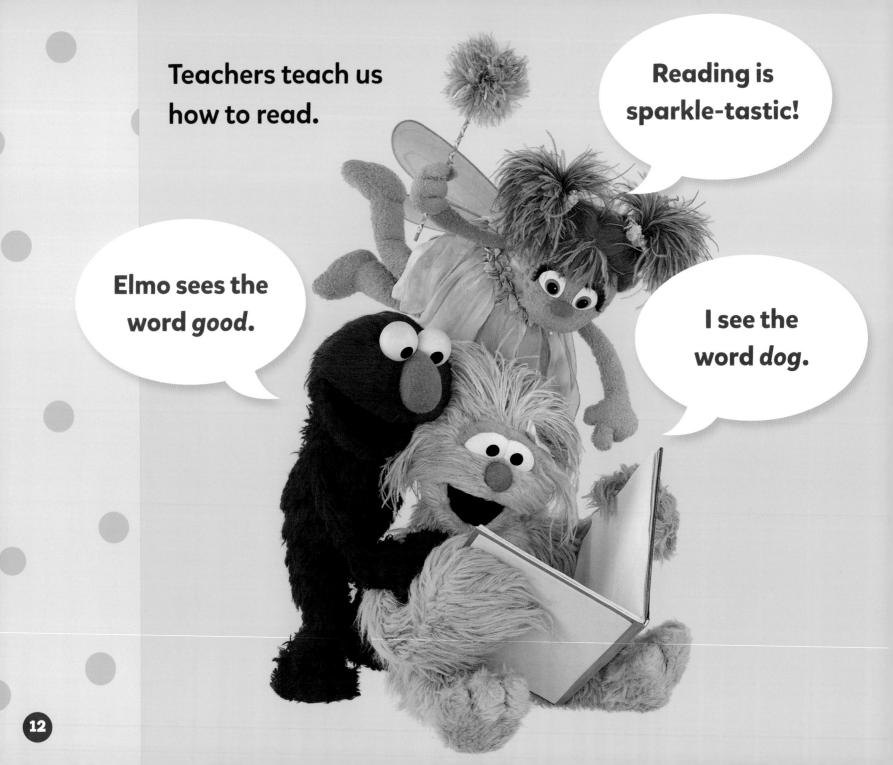

We read a lot of books.

Teachers teach us how to spell words.

I wrote a story about my best friend, Snuffy.

Writing lets us share our own stories.

Teachers help us learn about our world. They show us how plants grow.

I love learning about new plants for my garden!

They tell us about space.

Teachers teach us numbers. They teach us how to count.

Me like counting cookies.

We learn about shapes and colors.

Some teachers might work with just one or two students.

Julia has a special teacher at school.

Yay teachers!

They give the students special help.

Music teachers help us make music.

Phys ed teachers keep us moving.

Librarians teach in the library.

They teach us how to find answers to almost any question.

Teachers are patient. They know learning something new takes time.

Me like to learn how to make cookies!

They show us how to work together as a team.

Now it's your turn. Write a thank-you letter to your favorite teacher.

Dear Teacher,

Thank you for helping me learn. Thank you for cheering me on when I try something new. I am excited to keep learning.

Your friend,

Zoe

Picture Glossary

classroom: a room where teachers work with students

community: a place where people live and work

patient: calm and understanding

students: people who are learning things

Read More

Evans, Shira. *Helpers in Your Neighborhood.* Washington, DC: National Geographic Kids, 2018.

Heos, Bridget. *Teachers in My Community.* Minneapolis: Lerner Publications, 2019.

Waxman, Laura Hamilton. *Teacher Tools.* Minneapolis: Lerner Publications, 2020.

Index

Photo Acknowledgments

Additional image credits: Image Source/Getty Images, p. 5; Caiaimage/Robert Daly/Getty Images, pp. 6, 30; monkeybusinessimages/Getty Images, p. 7; lawcain/Getty Images, p. 8; Ariel Skelley/Getty Images, pp. 9, 30; ma nonallard/Getty Images, p. 10; JohnnyGreig/Getty Images, p. 11; FatCamera/Getty Images, pp. 13, 21–22; Jose Luis Pelaez Inc/Getty Images, pp. 14, 16; Jamie Grill/Getty Images, p. 15; SDI Productions/Getty Images, pp. 17, 29; JGI/Jamie Grill/Getty Images, p. 18; Monkey Business Images/Shutterstock.com, pp. 19–20, 30; Alistair Berg/Getty Images, p. 23; JBryson/Getty Images, p. 24; Wavebreakmedia/Getty Images, p. 25; michaeljung/Shutterstock.com, pp. 26, 30; SolStock/Getty Images, p. 27.

Cover: monkeybusinessimages/Getty.

Lerner Publications Company
An imprint of Lerner Publishing Group, Inc.
241 First Avenue North
Minneapolis, MN 55401 USA

For reading levels and more information, look up this title at www.lernerbooks.com.

Main body text set in Mikado Medium.
Typeface provided by HVD Fonts.

Editor: Allison Juda **Designer:** Emily Harris **Photo Editor:** Rebecca Higgins
Lerner team: Martha Kranes

Library of Congress Cataloging-in-Publication Data

Names: Boothroyd, Jennifer, 1972- author.
Title: All about teachers / Jennifer Boothroyd.
Description: Minneapolis : Lerner Publications, [2021] | Series: Sesame Street loves community
    helpers | Includes bibliographical references and index. | Audience: Ages 4–8 | Audience: Grades
    K–1 | Summary: "Elmo loves his teachers! They help make his community smarter, stronger, and
    kinder. Favorite Sesame Street Muppets invite you along to learn all about teachers in this friendly
    approach to key-curricular content"— Provided by publisher.
Identifiers: LCCN 2019035818 (print) | LCCN 2019035819 (ebook) | ISBN 9781541589940 (library
    binding) | ISBN 9781728400969 (ebook)
Subjects: LCSH: Teachers—Juvenile literature.
Classification: LCC LB1775 .B584 2021 (print) | LCC LB1775 (ebook) | DDC 371.102—dc23

LC record available at https://lccn.loc.gov/2019035818
LC ebook record available at https://lccn.loc.gov/2019035819

Manufactured in the United States of America
1-47504-48048-11/7/2019